W9-DES-009

Dream Catcher
The Legend, The Lady, The Woman

By Karen Hartman

To Mrs. Macumber &
Third Grade Class.
May you find beauty within hearts
& open your eyes and
Learn to feel the words and dreams
and share your knowledge.
As more will come to you —
Happy Dreams!
Karen G.
10/14/95

Illustrations by
Louise Bussière

WEEPING HEART PUBLICATIONS

Campbellsport, WI 53010

Ordering Information

Weeping Heart Publications

N1634 Lakeshore Drive

Campbellsport, WI 53010

(414) 533-8880

ISBN 0-9635204-1-5

Library of Congress Number 94-060140

Cataloging in Publication Data.
Hartman, Karen L.

Dream Catcher - The Legend, The Lady, The Woman / By Karen L. Hartman;
illustrated by Louise Bussière
        [72] p. : ill. 28 cm.

Summary: An adaptation of an Ojibwa Indian legend about a dream catcher that entangles bad dreams in the webbing and allows only the good dreams to go through. The Dream Catcher Lady goes through the steps of making a dream catcher comparing it to the journey of life. She shows people the importance of being themselves as well as sharing and learning from each other. Continue as she emerges as the Dream Catcher Woman becoming older and wiser.
        (398.2/097 or E)
1. Ojibwa Indians - Legends. 2. Spiders - Fiction. 3. Dreams - Fiction.
4. Self-perception. 5. Self-respect. I. Louise Bussière, ill. II. Title
III. Title: The Dream Catcher Lady.

Printed on recycled paper

Printed in the United States of America

HM Graphics - Printing - West Allis, WI

Dedication

To my parents, Ted and Signe Hill, who gave me life.

To my husband Dave and our children Kadee, David, Ted and their families who are a large part of my life.

To everyone who has touched my life in anyway, past, present and future.

A 'Special' Thank You to everyone who gave me their support the second time around.

- Karen

To my children, to my grandchildren...

Remember, all you will ever need, you have been

given...

A spirit within that describes you as love...

And a heart capable of the courage to discover this.

-Louise

4

Boo-zhoo' (Hello)

Who Am I?

I am me.
I am a woman of many nations.
I am not you.
I am not him.
I am not her,
Even though I thought I wanted to be.
But I am the daughter
Of my father and mother.
I am the sister of my brothers and sisters.
I am the wife of my husband.
I am the mother of our children.
I am a person who has much to give,
And who will find a way to give it.
I am me.
I am

The Dream Catcher Lady!

I'm always asked how I got
my name. Many years ago, while
watching an Ojibwa elder making a web
in a hoop, I asked, "What are you making?"
She replied, "I am making a Dream Catcher."

The Ojibwa elder explained that a Dream Catcher is a hoop with
spider-like webbing in the center and feathers hanging from the
bottom. It is used to catch your dreams. As she was teaching me how to
make the web, she told me the legend of the Dream Catcher.

7

"Dreams", she explained, "have always had many meanings to the Native Americans. One of the old Ojibwa traditions is to hang a Dream Catcher in their home. They believe that the night air is full of dreams, both good and bad. A Dream Catcher when hung moves freely in the air and catches the dreams as they float by."

8

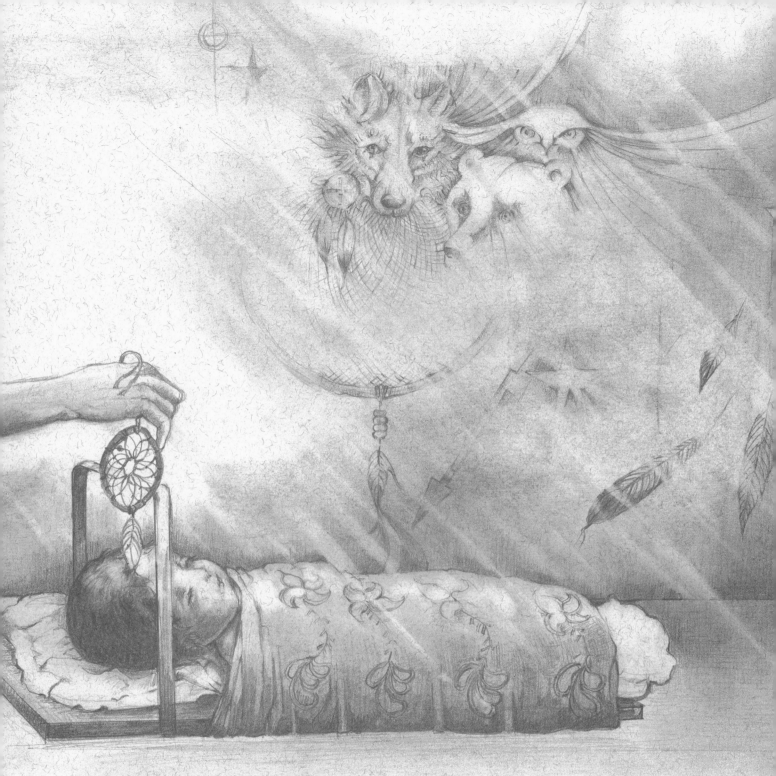

"The good dreams know their way and will go through the center hole, sliding down off the soft feather so gently that the sleeper below does not know he is dreaming."

"The bad dreams, not knowing the way, get entangled in the webbing and perish with the first light of the new day."

"Small Dream Catchers are hung on cradleboards so infants will have good dreams. Other sizes are hung for all to have good dreams."

9

I asked the elder if she knew how the Dream
Catchers came to be. She replied, "There
are many stories my people have
told and retold over many,
many generations.

I am sure they have
changed, for they have been told
and retold many times from the
grandmothers to their children and
grandchildren. This is one story that my
grandmother told when I was a little girl. It is called
    'The Old Woman and The Trickster'."

Now everyone knows that the Spider is a
trickster and will do many things to play tricks on
humans. There seems to be no limit to how much time
and trouble he will go through to play a trick on my people.
Once he placed a dry twig under some leaves, so when a
young hunter stepped on it, the cracking sound scared off the deer
he had been stalking all day.

Another time, a young girl was picking berries with her mother. The best berries were across the creek. As the young girl was crossing the creek, carefully stepping on the stones, the Spider placed some moss on a stone causing her to slip and fall into the water.

Everyone always knew who caused these accidents, but they were helpless to avoid them. The Trickster would laugh to himself each time he played one of his tricks on my people. Spiders always laugh to themselves. We know this is true because no one has heard a spider laugh out loud, no matter how funny he thinks he is.

One day an Old Woman was gathering wood for her fire, thinking about her many grandchildren and how she enjoyed playing with them and telling them stories. She sighed as she thought about how sad it was that children sometimes had bad dreams. While she picked through the wood for sticks to burn, an idea about dreams came to her.

16

After looking all around,

The Old Woman finally

found what she was seeking, the

Spider's home, which was built beside the big marsh near some cattails. The Old

Woman then caught a fly that was buzzing near her head and placed it in the Spider's

web. As the fly was struggling to free itself, the Spider came out to see what was

causing his home to shake.

"Good Morning," The Old Woman said to the Trickster. "See the present that I have brought you?" Spiders are not used to humans being nice to them, so he ran to the edge of his web and peeked out from under a leaf.

The Old Woman again spoke, "I have brought you this gift in thanks for the many times you have helped me." This made the Trickster very curious, for he would never make life easier for humans.

The Old Woman lied to the Spider. She explained that as a very lazy young girl she had hated to help her mother. She thanked the Spider for the time he made the great winds to come, causing much of the wild rice growing in the marsh to fall into the water. Now, the women of the village could not gather the wild rice for their winter food supply. That had saved much work!

This made the Spider giggle to himself, for he had always felt that had been one of his best tricks. He slowly crawled out from under the leaf so he could hear the woman speak more clearly.

22

The Old Woman then told
of how the Spider had
shown the Bear where her
mother's favorite berry patch was, so when her mother wanted her to help pick berries,
they were all gone! (This also was not true, of course. She had enjoyed helping her
mother gather berries because the women would tell stories and laugh. They also left
some berries for the bears and the birds to eat.)

25

She then offered to help the Trickster in return for his kindness to her. She said she would make hoops of red osier and, if the Spider would teach her to make webs like his for the hoops, she would hang the webbed hoops in her village. The Old Woman promised to bring all the trapped insects to the Spider's home, making his life easier.

The Spider thought and thought but could find no reason why the idea wasn't a good one. He could even tell the other spiders how he had tricked a human into helping him build webs and bring him food. At the thought of this plan he laughed so hard it made his home shake and shake.

While the Spider was thinking, The Old Woman found and cut a red osier branch that grew near the marsh and made a hoop of it. She returned to the Spider's home, bringing him another fly. This pleased the Spider, and he began showing the woman how to build a web inside the hoop. The Spider was a good teacher, as it turned out, because he made the woman take her web apart and reweave it many times. Finally, as the sun was beginning to go down, she completed a web that met with the Spider's approval.

The Old Woman again thanked the Spider for the tricks he had played on her village and promised to bring all the insects she caught in her webs. With this she hurried home, singing a happy song.

The next day the woman awoke early and gathered several red osier branches for hoops. She returned home and began her work, singing a happy song. To make the webbing she used sinew, knowing that insects would not be trapped in it. She was careful to follow the Spider's instructions on everything else. She made enough of the webbed hoops for every lodge in her village. Then she gathered the people around her and told them her story.

The Old Woman told the people to take the webbed hoops to their lodges and hang them from the lodge poles above their sleeping robes. She reminded them that spiders never had nightmares because their bad dreams became entangled in their webbing, and now the people could catch their bad dreams with their own Dream Catcher.

The Old Woman explained that the good dreams would find their way to the center hole and drift down to the sleeping person.

, she said, if ever an insect should
ome entangled in the web, the people must
e it to the Spider. The village people all laughed and
ghed because The Old Woman had tricked the Trickster.

After listening to the legend and the story of The Old Woman and The Trickster, I wanted a Dream Catcher for myself, but the elder could not provide me with one, for she had none completed.

She said, "I have shown you how to make Dream Catchers and we have shared many thoughts and feelings. With this knowledge you will become a Dream Catcher Lady because of your spirit you hold inside." She smiled at me and turned to her work, bending and binding the red osier while softly chanting an Ojibwa cradle song.

It was the end of a wonderful visit, and I knew it would be a time I remembered. For that brief time we shared, I give her thanks. She is one of the many people who have shared their gifts of knowledge with me, so that I may pass them on to you.

I went on with my life, but remembered the beauty of the
legend and our brief meeting.
As time passed, I found myself trying to make a Dream Catcher.
After several attempts, I thought I knew all, but after years of just making
and sharing them, I began to realize what was meant by the Ojibwa elder's
teaching. It came with the help of friends and people I've met.

While I was sharing the love of the Dream Catcher, I became "The Dream Catcher
Lady". This did not happen overnight but was nurtured as a baby before a mother gives
birth.

Too many times in our lives we take things for granted and do not appreciate things
around us. We see only what we want. We are upset when judged by others, but
forget that we, too, may have judged.

I share my gift of knowledge of Native Americans through
presentations.
I love to give as much as I can, and continue to learn so I can give
more.
I find myself trying to find ways of reaching more people, so they
have a better understanding of how the Native Americans learned
to use what nature provided. My goal is to open eyes and hearts
to better understanding all cultures and to see how we have
learned from each other.

What I hold close to my heart provided many answers. I found
beauty within the Dream Catcher. It has helped me to show
people the importance of being themselves, to have a clear
mind and open heart. Each step that I take in making a
Dream Catcher has meaning and will help each person to
find the ME inside of them. So come and join me on my
journey of making a Dream Catcher.

I gather the special branches of red osier in the spring of the year when new life is being born and existing life is awakening. I hand-select the branches, for not all branches want to be a Dream Catcher; they are all different, just like people. Each Dream Catcher has its own personality as it takes on its shape.

The joining of the ends to complete the circle symbolizes a "healing point". When people have a broken spirit because they were offended or have offended someone, their spirit is small. When they are helping or sharing, their spirit is large. People can become larger or smaller in spirit, just as the hoop is adjustable. In life one must learn to adjust and to live in balance and harmony.

The hoop symbolizes many things: our Creator, the Sacred Circle of birth-life-death, the bond between man and woman, the Earth's seasons, and our own spirit of individuality.

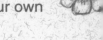

I weave a web when in good spirit like the trickster spider except using sinew for the webbing. The web represents life's ups and downs and the different paths we take in life.

We must remember when our spirits are down, the simplest compliment is an 'up'. That is the time to remember the things that make us happy and important! Life is meaningful and we must believe in ourselves. We must learn to build up our self-esteem and to help others to do the same.

A gift does not need to be wrapped in a pretty package with ribbons and bows. Even when someone offends us, that is a gift, not to be like them. A gift also comes from the person who shares knowledge and a helping hand.

We will take many paths in life. When we take the wrong one, learn from it, just as we find joy and happiness from the right paths.

Into the Dream Catcher's webbing I weave a red 'white heart' bead. The red 'white heart' bead is my spirit bead, my way of leaving something of myself behind.

As in the legend, the center is left open so the good dreams can go through, while the bad dreams become entangled in the webbing.

47

The feathers I use for the dreams to slide down are from unendangered legal birds. We must protect the birds that are endangered. When we look at the feathers, think of the eagles, owls, hawks and other birds of prey. Think of their beauty in flight and how there is beauty within us all and how we, too, need to learn to let our spirits soar.

Think of their keen eyesight and alertness and how we need to learn to LOOK and SEE. We SEE what is in front of us, but need to LOOK for the who, what and why. The more we learn to LOOK and the more we begin to SEE, the more we can begin to share and grow.

49

To the feathers I have added four glass beads - yellow, red, black and white. The beads represent the four directions, the four seasons, and the four colors of mankind ... the caretakers of Mother Earth.

When the Dream Catcher is completed,
I remind myself that the key to
happiness is something we all
uniquely hold, for it is kept in our
HEARTS.

The Dream Catcher is now ready to be
given, to be a source of beauty from
within itself and the source of all. . .

HAPPY DREAMS!!!!

DREAM CATCHER WOMAN

(Dedicated to The Dream Catcher Lady)

Old Weaver Woman
Weave baby a web
Of golden and silver
Of life's silken thread

Bring baby sweet visions
Under Grandmother moon
Bring baby sweet dreams
Within sacred hoop

Hush, hush little baby
Hear the song of the night
Hear the wind gently calling
Through the circle of life

Wē, Wē little baby
Let your spirit take flight
For Dream Catcher Woman
Blesses your night

by Yolanda Barch

The path to becoming a Dream Catcher Woman is not an easy one. But it has opened my eyes to know I must continue on my journey so I can share my knowledge. Since we all have so much to share and learn, we must learn how to share and communicate.

Sharing has helped me reach another rung in the ladder of success, but lack of communication has made me feel as though I were falling. Now it is time to pull my strength together from the people who care and from the feelings that I hold inside.

As we grow older, we grow wiser; we become foolish only if we let ourselves. We must learn to keep our eyes open and communicate so our downs in life will be fewer and our ups will grow higher.

When we share our knowledge with others, we not only grow, but we help others to grow. They, in turn, will help someone else. Think of the wonderful garden we are creating and cultivating.

59

We must keep our eyes open, since the
four directions have so much to show us.
The four seasons have so much to share.
Most important are the people. As I continue
on my journey of life, I keep my eyes, ears and
heart open, for we can see only what is on the
surface and need to learn to see more.

Some day our paths will cross, as we are all........

DREAM CATCHERS.

Glossary

Colors: The colors used do not represent any individual tribe. Depending on the time period and traditions, individual adaptations did occur. The colors are used as symbols to promote a better understanding; to help people live in balance and harmony.

Yellow: East, Spring, Asian: Keeper of the Air
Red: South, Summer, Native American: Keeper of the Earth
Black: West, Fall, African American: Keeper of the Water
White: North, Winter, Caucasian: Keeper of the Fire

Elder: A person who is older and wiser

Endangered Bird: Birds that are protected under the law

Legal Feathers: Ones that can be purchased

Ojibwa: A Chippewa, member of the Algonquian Linguistic group. Woodland Indians of the Great Lakes.

Osier: Any member of related willow, whose wood is used for baskets

Self-esteem: Belief in ones self, self respect

Sinew: A cord that fastens muscles to bones

Spirit Bead: Personal bead chosen to represent my signature

Wē-Wē: Swing, Swing

White Heart: Also known as Hudson Bay or Cornaline D'Aleppo

TO MY READERS

This is NOT just a children's book, but a book written for everyone. It can be read by or to everyone young at HEART! It is a way of giving back what has been given to me. I hope it will also be used as a guide for finding the ME inside everyone of you or to help someone else to find their ME.

In your lifetime you have to wear many hats. At times you may wish that you were someone else, but you never look at yourself as a whole person. You see only the side that you want to see. You do not think of the good in yourself; too many times you see only your negative side.

You must learn to live in balance and in harmony with all living things, including yourself. There is so much that you can learn - quite often this is right in front of your eyes. And you have so much to share - many times you do not realize the worth or importance of your knowledge. Remember we are all a seed in our creator's garden. When you share you are planting a seed, nurtured by your knowledge, as water to make the seed grow. When that person looks for more information, that seed is growing. The more knowledge gained the seed will blossom and then flower. When that person starts to share all the knowledge gained he will begin creating another garden to watch grow.

When you read "Think About It", you may have additional statements, or questions you may want to add. Write them on the pages entitled "Personal Notes". These "Think About It" statements are there to help guide you personally, or they can be used for group discussions. After you have read the entire passage concentrate on each statement, then encourage others to share their feelings with you.

Native Americans share legends by telling stories that were passed down from generation to generation, just as with many other cultures. Read the book, then retell the story by only looking at the pictures. Encourage the children to write stories about the pictures that they see. Storytelling is very important and we should encourage it.

I would like to thank everyone who has helped me. And helped me! This book has come to life because of everyone. I know this book will be enjoyed by all, young and old alike, for years to come. Keep the legend of the "Dream Catcher" alive.

Remember! Set your goals high and go after your Dreams! . . . . .   **Mi-gwetch' (Thank You)**

Karen

THINK ABOUT IT

Learn to spell can't without the "t".

The tone of your voice says a lot.

It's not what you do - It's how you do it.

Learn to take control of your life.

Name calling is a reflection of the person calling the names.

Attitude is choice - Attitude is important.

Words are only as powerful as we make them.

Be thankful for the joy one has given.

Be thankful for the knowledge one has shared.

We need competition in our lives. Winning is a good feeling!

When we lose we should think of how we can improve.

Don't take things for granted. Don't take life for granted.

If you have a problem with someone - talk it over with them, not everyone else.

Use your best communication skills, when working with others.

Envy is not healthy.

We are rough on the outside and shining on the inside.

We must learn to enjoy the little things in life - For there are so many of them.

Don't search for faults. Share knowledge.

There is a rainbow after every storm. Sometimes we just don't see it, so, close your eyes and imagine it.

No Guts - No Glory!

In times of sadness you'll find peace, if you search.

Gentle words will work better than harsh ones.

To make your dreams a reality, you have to act upon them.

We are not born prejudiced but learn it.

When you love someone, you love them as they are.

Life is like an onion. You peel off one layer at a time and sometimes you weep.

Children need role models and encouragement.

Things do not change. We do.

A child's heart is full of love and needs to be nurtured with each passing day.

Laughter is the best medicine.

Wealth is what we are, not what we have.

Discover what is important in your life before a crisis occurs.

Don't just listen to someone - understand what they are saying.

When you start something - finish it or give it to someone else to finish.

The smile you give, may be the smile that is remembered.

You can be the person you want to be.

We will all struggle in life - learn from it.

Everyone needs challenges - just as everyone needs failures.

Take a few moments for yourself everyday.

Be the first to forgive and your friendship will grow stronger.

Everything has a purpose - sometimes we just don't see it.

The art of healing is forgiving.

Every child needs love to grow - we never stop being that child.

We had NO choice of who we are, but we DO have a choice of who we will become.

Children are our future - treat them with respect.

Don't keep things bottled up inside - it's best to let it go.

You can accomplish anything you want in life, but first you have to <u>want</u> to do it.

Personal Notes

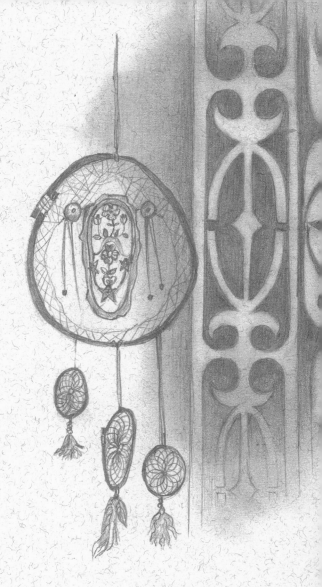

How to Make a Simple Dream Catcher

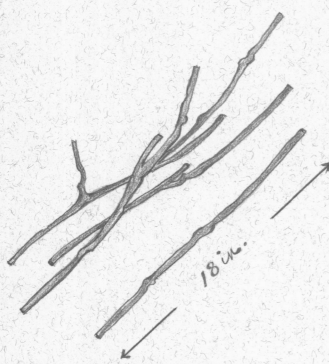

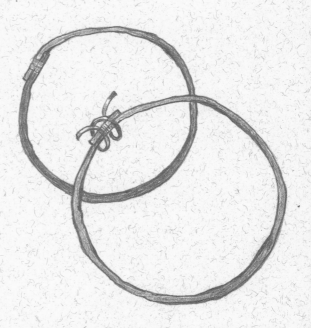

Overlap 1 1/2", tape to hold and wrap with
sinew* and tie off.

Gather young branches, saplings, or suckers.
Cut at 18 inches or your desired length.

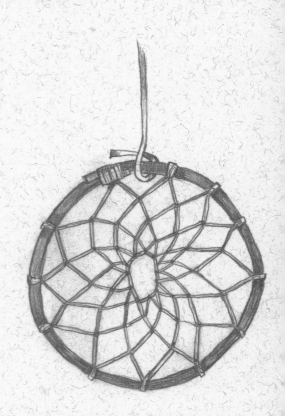

Continue to web working in a spiral. The
spans will become smaller. Continue until you
have the desired opening. Tie a knot at the
center and cut off remaining sinew.

Look at your Dream Catcher and decide wher
the top is. Tie a piece of sinew for the hanger

Note: If you have a hard time webbing or working with children, let
them wrap however they feel like doing it. Remember you had to cra
before you could walk. If you want to learn to web, you must learn to
have patience and to keep trying....

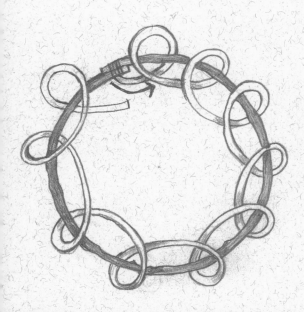

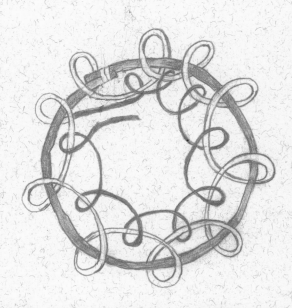

Cut a 5 yard piece of sinew and tie to the hoop. Make 10 (or whatever desired number of) evenly spaced half-hitches around the hoop.

Continue to web, half-hitching OVER the sinew spanning between the first row. Keep your sinew taut as you web.

For the LEFT-HANDER

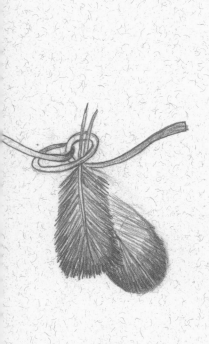

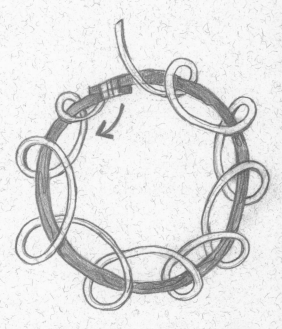

ut a 12" piece of sinew and tie 2 or 3 feathers the center. Thread beads onto sinew and ver the quills of the feathers, making sure the eads do not slide off the feathers. If that appens tie additional knots or add another eather. Tie onto the bottom of the Dream atcher.

* waxen linen, yarn, thread, any type of cordage can be used.

69

COMMENTS

Words can not express how deeply your wonderful book has touched my heart. There is magic within the pages. The words and artwork are woven together to create an object of beauty as delicate as a spider's web. The love shines out as brightly as the sun and warms the spirit within. Through the Dream Catcher the dreams of the heart have been realized into reality. So indeed, more magic has come to pass because of it, and a circle has been complete.

Yolanda Barch

When Karen appeared in our store, her book in hand, an aura of peace and warmth surrounded her. These feelings encouraged me to stop right then and read it. Beautifully written and charmingly illustrated, it is a book for all ages. Which imparts an ancient legend while sending a clear message for today. The author shares the truly important lessons of life - love, understanding, patience and mutual respect.

Judi Weil, Children's Coordinator
Audubon Court Books

Your book is one I would not be without. In fact, it is always within my reach to be read and re-read often. It is a thought provoking book for the young and the adult. The young will like the story and there is much in there that will start them thinking. The adult will experience deeper meanings, seemingly directed to oneself.
This book "touches" one. Something new and meaningful is found with every reading. One should have a dream catcher. Mine is a constant reminder of all this.

Lois Dean
Art Teacher

This book is truly a special gift - a gift of the heart, a sharing of the soul. It is so much more than just the re-telling of a legend. Karen encourages us to look within and beyond to see beauty, to create beauty, to feel life, and to touch spirit. Thank you, Karen, for sharing, for inspiring, and reminding us all of the way.

Linda Chalmers
Wing Song

Karen had a dream - a story to tell. Filled with a need to share her love, her knowledge, and her friendship this inspirational book was written. Louise read the words - put life into them, and graced every page with her beautiful drawings. My children, my grandchildren, Tom and I thank you for this timeless gift.

Gerry Lee Carroll

For information on the following, call or write to:

Karen Hartman
Weeping Heart Trading Company
N1634 Lakeshore Drive
Campbellsport, WI 53010

(414) 533-8880

Dream Catcher - The Legend, The Lady, The Woman
    by Karen Hartman - Illustrated by Louise Bussiére

Custom made Dream Catchers by Karen

Dream Catcher Kits designed by Karen

Assorted Dream Catcher Supplies
    Sinew, feathers, glass crow beads, reed, and fetishes

The Dream Catcher Collection:
    For the uniqueness and individuality of one of a kind art
    Dream Catchers with meanings - Honor Our Future - Our Children, Walks Together, Shield of
    Protection, United, Birth of a Dream, Even the Smallest Dreams Can Come True, Suspended
    Dreams, and other one-of-a-kind art.

Earth-Peace Friendship Bracelets designed by Karen
    To Honor - Mother Earth, Father Sky, the four directions, the four seasons, and the four colors
    of mankind --- caretakers of Mother Earth.

Assorted Dream Catchers and hand painted leather pillows by Kadee Woods

Dream Catcher Seminars and Presentations:
    "Finding Beauty Within", A motivational presentation focusing on the Dream Catcher.
    Presentations on Native Americans for pre-schoolers to senior citizens.
    How deer are used today and how they were used in past years.
    Showing and sharing how things were used that Mother Nature provided, beadwork, quillwork,
    basketry, rawhide, etc.
    A presentation on how to self-publish your own book from start to finish.

Beadwork Classes - Private or group lessons available - Lazystitch, applique, loomwork, heddle
loomwork, freehand loomwork, beadweaving, peyote stitch, gourd stitch and beaded jewelry.

Czechoslovakian Seed Beads, beading supplies, assorted beads and related items.

BIOGRAPHY

Karen Hartman was born and raised in San Gabriel, California and currently living in Wisconsin. She was taught the art of creating the Dream Catcher by an Ojibwa elder. She found beauty within the Dream Catcher, which helps one to find beauty and peace within one's self. Friends encouraged her to write her first book, <u>Dream Catcher - The Legend and The Lady</u>. Her continued growth and journey has created her second beautiful book, <u>Dream Catcher - The Legend, The Lady, The Woman</u>.

Karen has created many unique and inspiring Dream Catchers, some as small as 3/8 inch to as large as 36 inches. Her Dream Catchers are found throughout the United States and have found homes in museums in Rome, Holland, Germany, Switzerland, Guatemala, Austria, Africa, Japan, and the Philippines.

Louise Bussiére has been a professional artist since 1972 and has received over 200 regional and national awards. She is a published poetess, her poetry reflects the same time-suspended, mystical mood as her paintings do.

Louise has made the words of this book come alive with the beauty of her artwork.